The Mystery of the PB & J Jam

by M. J. Cosson

Perfection Learning®

Cover and Inside Illustrations: Michael A. Aspengren

For information, contact
Perfection Learning® Corporation,
1000 North Second Avenue, P.O. Box 500,
Logan, Iowa 51546-0500.
Tel: 1-800-831-4190
Fax: 1-712-644-2392
Paperback ISBN 0-7891-5255-x
Cover Craft® ISBN 0-7807-9669-1
4 5 6 7 8 PP 08 07 06 05

Table of Contents

Introduction

Abe, Ben, Gabe, Toby, and Ty live in a large city. There isn't much for kids to do. There isn't even a park close by.

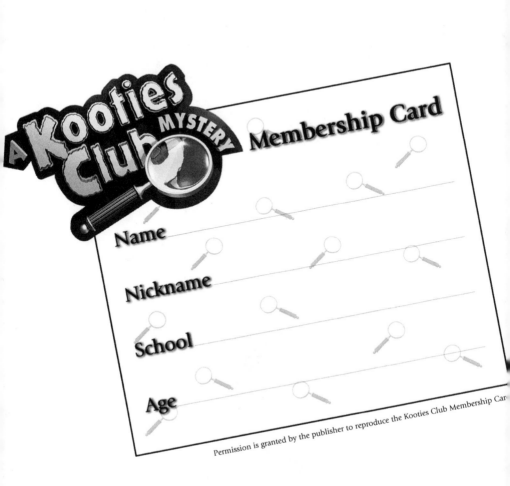

A **Kooties Club** MYSTERY

Membership Card

Name

Nickname

School

Age

Their neighborhood is made up of apartment houses and trailer parks. Gas stations and small shops stand where the parks and grass used to be. And there aren't many houses with big yards.

Ty and Abe live in an apartment complex. Next door is a large vacant lot. It is full of brush, weeds, and trash. A path runs across the lot. On the other side is a trailer park. Ben and Toby live there.

Across the street from the trailer park is a big gray house. Gabe lives in the top apartment of the house.

The five boys have known one another since they started school. But they haven't always been friends.

The other kids say the boys have cooties. And the other kids won't touch them with a ten-foot pole. So Abe, Ben, Gabe, Toby, and Ty have formed their own club. They call it the Kooties Club.

Here's how to join. If no one else will have anything to do with you, you're in.

The boys call themselves the Koots for short. Ben's grandma calls his grandpa an *old coot*. And Ben thinks his grandpa is pretty cool. So if he's an old coot, Ben and his friends must be young koots.

The Koots play ball and hang out with one another. But most of all, they look for mysteries to solve.

Chapter 1

Nothing to Do

Toby stuck the knife in the jar. He pulled out a glob of peanut butter. He spread it on the bread. He scraped the rest off the knife with his finger. He licked the peanut butter off his finger.

Then Toby stuck the knife in the grape jelly jar. He spread the jelly on the other piece of bread. Then he slapped the two pieces together.

"Here." He handed it to Gabe.

He made one for himself. Now each Koot had a PB & J sandwich. The salty taste of peanut butter mixed with the sweet jelly taste. What could be better? The Koots all chewed away.

That is, all but Ty.

The boys had tall glasses of chocolate milk too. They gulped the sweet, cold milk between bites of PB & J.

That is, all but Ty.

Ty couldn't eat peanut butter. And he couldn't drink milk. There were lots of things Ty couldn't have.

"If you ever go to jail, you won't mind the food," Gabe said.

Ty was eating plain bread. And drinking water.

11

"Yeah," Ty said. "The food there can't be worse than what I eat all the time."

"That's why you're so skinny," Toby said. He looked down at his own round stomach. He wondered if he could get a food allergy.

"I'm not skinny," Ty said. "I'm just right. You're fat."

"I'm not fat," Toby said. "I'm plump. But you *are* skinny."

Ben looked at them both. "Ty, you're skinny," he said. "And, Toby, you're fat. So what else is new?"

Gabe took a deep breath. "Skinny, fat," he said. "Don't we have anything better to talk about? Let's do something."

"I know," Abe said. "We could act like some of us are in prison. And some could be the guards. We could have bread and water."

The Koots just looked at him.

"That's really lame, Abe," Toby said. Everybody agreed.

"We need a mystery," Ben said. Everybody agreed again.

13

Chapter 2

Emergency!

The next day at school, there was a party. The Popco people had given the whole school big tins of popcorn. Each tin had a different kind of popcorn. Some tasted like cheese. Some tasted like candy. Some tasted like fruit. There was soda pop to drink too.

At 3:00, everybody went to the lunchroom. All the tins were opened. Each student got a can of soda pop and a paper bag. A plastic cup was placed in each tin. Students used the cup to scoop popcorn into their bags. They got to eat as much popcorn as they wanted.

At 3:30 the party was over. The Koots met at the door. They started to walk home.

"I sure could use some candy," Gabe said.

"We just had all that popcorn," Ben said.

"I'm sick of popcorn," said Abe. "And it never fills me up."

"Me neither," Toby said.

"And I didn't eat much," Ty said. "Does anybody have money?"

The Koots stopped. They checked their pockets. They counted their money. Ben added it all up. They had enough to buy a bag of suckers.

"Let's go to the Stop 'n Shop," Ben said.

Outside the Stop 'n Shop, Toby tore open the bag. Each Koot took two suckers. They tore off the wrappers. They walked along the street. Each Koot had two suckers in his mouth. They couldn't talk.

It was quiet for a few minutes. The Koots walked along.

Then Ty took his suckers out of his mouth.

16

"My mouth feels funny," he said. His voice was strange.

Abe took his suckers out. "Mine does too," he said. "Orange and lime aren't very good together. I think I'll have one at a time." He put the lime one back in.

Ben took his suckers out. "Cherry and lime are good together," he said. He stuck both suckers back in his mouth.

The Koots walked on.

Ty gasped.

Thud! Ty fell to the sidewalk. His friends bent over him. He had blotches on his skin. His eyes were closed. His tongue stuck out of his mouth. He looked dead.

One of the Koots screamed, "Help!"

17

Several cars passed by. No one noticed the Koots.

Suddenly, a car stopped. A man jumped out. He had green hospital clothes on. "I'm a doctor," he said.

The man bent over Ty. He put his ear to Ty's mouth.

"What happened?" the man asked.

"He just dropped to the ground," Toby replied.

"Does he have any allergies?" the doctor asked.

"Yeah," Gabe answered. "He can't eat peanut butter. But he hasn't had any."

"Grab that bag from the back seat!" he yelled.

Toby got the bag.

"Run to that store and call 911," said the man.

19

Ben and Gabe took off for the store.

The man took something from the bag. He pushed up Ty's sleeve. Then he jabbed a needle into Ty's arm. The doctor gave Ty a shot!

Abe and Toby looked away. Toby thought he would faint.

The man put his bag under Ty's feet.

"Grab that jacket from my car," he ordered.

Toby got the jacket. The man threw it over Ty.

Ty just lay there. His suckers had fallen out of his mouth. They lay beside him. All Abe and Toby could do was wait—and hope.

Chapter 3

What Happened?

At last, the ambulance came. The medics put Ty in the ambulance.

"Go to his house. Give his parents this card," the man in green said to the Koots. He wrote something on the back.

"Please come with us." The doctor took Gabe by the arm and led him toward the waiting ambulance.

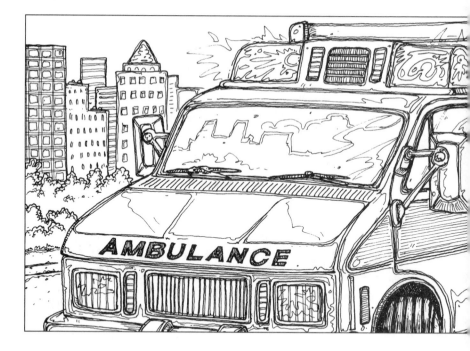

They got into the ambulance. It sped off. The man left his car on the street.

Ben, Abe, and Toby looked at the card. It read, "Dr. Henry Moss." On the back, Dr. Moss had written, "Come to Children's Hospital."

"Ty's mom won't be home from work yet," Abe said.

"Let's go to your place, Abe," Ben said. "Your mom will be home. Maybe she'll know how to reach Ty's mom."

The Koots ran all the way to Abe's apartment.

They ran into the apartment. They were out of breath.

"Mom!" yelled Abe. "Ty's sick! We need to get his mom!"

Abe's mom was on the phone.

"Gotta go," she said. She put the phone down.

"What?"

Abe gave his mom the card. "Ty is very sick. He might even be dead. We called the ambulance. This doctor stopped. He gave Ty a shot. They took Ty in the ambulance. The doctor and Gabe went too," he said.

His mom was already looking in the phone book. She dialed a number.

"I'll get Ty's mom," she said. "Then I'll call Gabe's mom."

Abe, Toby, and Ben all looked at one another. Their eyes were big.

"I wonder what happened to Ty," Ben said.

Abe's mom got off the phone.

"Ty's mom is on her way to the hospital," she said.

"What happened?" asked Abe.

"I bet it was a food allergy," Toby said.

"I've seen Ty get bumps on his skin from food," Ben said. "But nothing like this."

"Maybe he had a heart attack," Abe said. "Kids can have them."

"No," Toby said. "I bet it was food."

"What food?" asked Ben. "Popcorn, candy, lunch?"

"We wanted a mystery," Toby said. "But not like this."

25

Chapter 4

Ty's Troubles

When Gabe got back, he didn't have much news. The people at the hospital had asked him Ty's name and address.

Gabe sat in a waiting room for a long time. He didn't get to see Ty. After a while, his mom picked him up and took him home.

None of the Koots slept well that night. They were worried about their pal.

At last, morning came. Abe asked if he had to go to school.

"Yes," said his mom. "I'll call the hospital. They'll tell me how Ty is."

She dialed the phone. Abe sat there as she asked about Ty. Soon she hung up.

"They say he will be there a day or two more," she said. "His mom is with him."

"Can the Koots go visit him?" asked Abe.

"No," said his mom. "But you can call him after school."

Every Koot's mom had called the hospital. They all had the number to reach Ty after school.

In class, Ben told the teacher what had happened. The class made cards for Ty.

27

The school day lasted forever. At last, 3:30 came. The Koots raced to Toby's house.

Ty lay in bed. He was in a room with three other kids. The phone rang. The biggest kid got it.

"It's for you, Ty," he said. He handed the phone to Ty.

" 'Lo?" Ty said.

"What happened?" Toby asked. Gabe grabbed the phone away.

"Are you okay?" he asked.

All the Koots were trying to get their ears on the phone. They all wanted to talk to Ty. Finally, Toby pushed the phone's speaker button.

"I'm okay now," Ty said. "They have me hooked up to an IV. I have to stay here another day."

28

"Hooked to a plant?" asked Abe.

"What plant?" asked Ty.

"Like an ivy plant," Abe said.

"No, it's the letters *I* and *V*. It's a needle in my arm. There's a bottle hanging upside down. It drips stuff in me through the needle."

"Yuck," Gabe said.

"What happened?" Toby asked again.

"I was in shock," Ty said.

"Like an electric shock?" asked Toby.

"No. Like my body shut down. It just quit working. It might have been something I ate," Ty said.

"I knew it," Toby said.

"Boy, you were lucky Dr. Moss came along," Ben said.

"Yeah, we didn't know what to do," Gabe said.

29

"It was scary," Abe said.

"How did you guys know about Dr. Moss?" asked Ty.

"We were all there when he stopped his car," Ben said.

"If he hadn't come along . . ." Gabe said. He stopped.

"What?" Ty said. "You mean I might be dead?"

Nobody said anything.

"I know," Ty said. "I don't remember anything. But I guess he did save my life."

The Koots on the other end of the phone all looked at one another. Their friend had almost died.

"I can't eat anything yet," Ty said.

"Wow," Abe said. "I bet you're hungry."

"A little," Ty said. "They're putting me on a diet."

The Koots all laughed. Ty didn't need a diet.

"I can only eat certain foods," Ty said.

"Will it help if we find the food that made you sick?" asked Ben.

"You can try," Ty said. "I know I can't eat any nuts or milk. But I was very careful yesterday. I only ate things I'd had before."

"Something must have been different," Toby said.

"We'll find out what," Gabe said.

"Thanks, guys," Ty said. "See you soon."

Chapter 5

Something to Do

"I wonder what kind of popcorn he ate," Ben said. "He said he had a little."

"He also said he didn't have anything he hadn't had before," Gabe said.

"We've all had those suckers before," Toby said.

"Maybe it was lunch," Abe said.

"We'd better check it all out," Ben said. He picked up his notebook from school. At the top of a page, he wrote *Ty's Foods.* Then he put yesterday's date.

Under that he wrote *Breakfast.*

"I guess we'll have to ask Ty's mom about breakfast," Ben said.

Then he wrote *Lunch.*

"He ate the school lunch," Gabe said.

"What was lunch yesterday?" asked Abe.

"I think it was hot dogs," Toby said.

"And chips. And carrot sticks. And peaches," Ben added.

"And a peanut butter cookie!" Abe said.

"He didn't eat his cookie," Toby said. "I ate it. I gave him my peaches."

"And he always has grape juice. Not milk," Ben said. He wrote everything down.

"Was there anything between lunch and the popcorn?" asked Ben.

"No," Toby answered.

"Yes," Gabe said. "I had some gum. Ty had a piece at recess."

"So did I," Toby said. "Could mint make Ty sick?"

"Better write it down," Ben said.

Popcorn. He wrote that down too. "Does anybody know what kind of popcorn Ty had?"

"I think just plain popcorn," Gabe said. "I was with him at the party. He didn't eat much. Just like he said. He

34

had a can of soda. I think he had root beer."

"Didn't Ty have two red suckers?" asked Ben.

"He had one red and one orange," Abe said. "I wanted the red one. But Ty got it first."

"That's it," Gabe said. "That's what he had. Now what?"

"Now we find out what's in all this stuff," Toby said.

35

Chapter 6

Ty Returns

The next day, the Kooties Club went on a hunt. They asked questions. They read labels. They wrote everything down. By the end of the day, they had many pages of notes.

After supper, the Koots met at Abe's. They walked upstairs to Ty's apartment. They rang the doorbell. Ty opened the door.

"Hey, guys," Ty said.

"You look skinny," Toby said. "Have you been on a diet?"

"Ha, ha," Ty said in a fake way. He walked slowly to a chair and sat down.

"I won't be in school for a while," Ty said. "We have to find out what happened to me."

"Here," Ben said. He held out the pages of notes.

"What's all this?" Ty asked.

"It's everything you ate the other day," Toby said.

"Yeah," Abe said. "We even found the suckers you dropped. We looked on all the labels. The lunchroom ladies helped us too. We even checked out the popcorn you ate." He smiled. "You did just have plain, right?"

37

"I can't remember," Ty said. "I think so.

"Sounds like you guys thought of everything," he said. "I'll give this to my mom. She can give it to the doctors."

"You got more than one doctor?" asked Abe.

"Yeah," Ty said. "Dr. Moss saved my life. But at the hospital, some other doctors looked at me."

"So what can you eat?" asked Toby.

"Not much," Ty said. "Just a few things that they know are okay. Every week, I'll get to try something new."

"Just like a baby," Gabe said.

"Do you feed yourself?" asked Toby.

Ty nodded. "Goo," he said.

38

Chapter 7

Not Again!

Ty came back to school the next week. Now he always brought a lunch from home. He didn't eat any school food. And he didn't eat anything at his friends' houses.

Some weeks went by. The doctors still didn't know what had made Ty sick. It was a mystery. Nobody wanted it to happen again. But the Koots didn't know how to solve it.

Now Ty wore a necklace. It told others what to do if he got sick. The necklace and his food were the only signs that Ty was sick. Otherwise, he seemed okay. He ran. He played ball. He joked around. The Koots almost forgot about Ty's problem.

One Saturday, the Koots sat on Gabe's porch. It was after lunch. Everyone had gone home to eat. Nobody ate PB & J around Ty anymore—just in case.

"Let's go see Mr. Dodge," Ben said. "Maybe he has some new stories for us to listen to."

Everybody nodded. They walked across the vacant lot.

Thud! Ty was lying on the ground. He was on his back. His eyes were closed.

40

Abe screamed, "Get help! Get help!"

Toby just stood there. He was too scared to move. No! Not again! he thought.

Gabe took off for his house. "I'll call 911," he yelled.

Ben grabbed Ty's necklace. He started to read it. Ty jerked. His legs jumped. Then his arms jumped. Then his eyes flew open. He started to laugh.

"Come back," Toby called to Gabe. "He's faking."

"You jerk," Ben said. "That's not funny."

"You guys should have seen yourselves," he said. Ty laughed and rolled on the ground.

Abe almost started to cry. "That was mean, Ty," he said. He turned his back. He started to walk home. He didn't want anybody to see his tears.

Toby said, "How could you?" He wanted to hit Ty. He turned to walk home.

Ben stood up. He just looked at Ty. He turned to walk home too. "Wait for me, Toby," he yelled.

Gabe had started back across the lot. The other Koots were walking

away from Ty. Ty still lay there laughing.

Gabe stopped. Ty was his best friend. He didn't want Ty to be sick. But Ty had played a mean joke. Gabe turned to walk back home.

Ty lay on the ground all alone. He kept laughing for a while. Then he stopped laughing. He lay looking up at the sky. Tears started to roll from his eyes.

Ty was sick. And now his friends were mad at him.

Chapter 8

All Alone

Ty spent the rest of Saturday in his apartment. He watched TV by himself. On Sunday, he saw the other Koots all go into Abe's. He walked out his front door. He started to walk downstairs. Before he could get to Abe's apartment, the Koots were heading outside. They ran toward the empty lot. Gabe had a ball.

"Hey, guys," Ty yelled. He waved.

Nobody said anything. They just kept running.

Ty stopped. He turned around. He walked back upstairs. He went back inside his apartment. He turned on the TV.

On Monday morning, Ty walked to school by himself. He walked home by himself Monday after school.

On Tuesday, he walked to and from school by himself. Ty spent all week alone. If the Koots saw Ty, they acted like he wasn't there.

By Friday, Ty wasn't worried that his friends were mad at him. He didn't have any friends.

45

On Saturday, Ty went to see Mr. Dodge. Mr. Dodge was homebound. He had been in a bad accident. He was in a wheelchair. And he had lost his sight.

The Koots liked to visit Mr. Dodge. He played books on tape for them. He had some good mysteries.

Mr. Dodge was good at solving mysteries too.

Ty didn't have a mystery. He had a problem. He thought maybe Mr. Dodge could help him solve it.

46

Chapter 9

Help from a Friend

Ring! Ben's mom picked up the phone.

"It's for you, Ben," she said. She handed Ben the phone.

" 'Lo," Ben said. He listened.

"Okay, we'll be there," he said. He hung up.

Ben called Gabe. "Come over," he said.

Gabe came to Ben's trailer. Then they walked to Toby's. They picked Abe up last. All the Koots headed for Mr. Dodge's apartment. They didn't stop to get Ty.

"What's up?" asked Abe.

"Mr. Dodge said he had a mystery," Ben said. "He said to come right over. Bring everybody."

They rang the bell.

"Come in. It's open," Mr. Dodge called.

The Koots went in. It was dark inside Mr. Dodge's apartment.

"Can I open the curtains?" asked Toby.

"Not right now," said Mr. Dodge. "Sit down, boys."

48

Mr. Dodge didn't sound very happy. The Koots sat down.

For a long time, nobody said anything.

At last, Ben said, "Is this about Ty?"

"This is about a mystery," said Mr. Dodge.

"You were helping to solve it. Then you stopped. Your friend still needs your help."

"He's not our friend," Toby said.

"He tricked us," Ben said.

"It was a mean trick," Abe said.

"He told me about it," said Mr. Dodge. "He's sorry."

"Too late for sorry," Gabe said. But he wasn't sure he really meant it.

"What does he want us to do? Have a party for him?" asked Ben.

49

"No," said Mr. Dodge. "He wants to have a party for you. To thank you for your help when he was sick. Will you come back here next Tuesday at 5 o'clock?"

The Koots all looked at one another. It was hard to see faces.

They were quiet for a while.

"Okay," Gabe said.

"Okay," Abe said.

"I guess so," Ben said.

"I'll think about it," Toby said.

"You'll be glad you did," said Mr. Dodge.

50

Chapter 10

Mystery Solved!

On Tuesday at 5 o'clock, the Koots rang Mr. Dodge's doorbell.

"Come on in. It's open."

The Koots went in. The curtains were open. Mr. Dodge sat in his wheelchair. Ty stood beside him. Across the room sat Dr. Moss.

"Hi, guys," said Dr. Moss.

"Hey," said the Koots all together.

Ty didn't say anything.

"Have a seat," said Mr. Dodge. Toby, Abe, Ben, and Gabe sat down. They looked at one another. They didn't look at Ty.

"I have something to say," Ty said.

The Koots still did not look at him.

Ty began, "I was wrong to play that trick. I don't know why I did it. It just came to me to fake it."

He looked down.

"It was a dumb thing to do. But something good came from it."

Ty cleared his throat. "It made you not like me. So then I didn't have any friends. I had time to think.

"It made me think about the day I got sick," Ty continued. "I went over and over what I'd had to eat. And I remembered something. Nobody knew this but me."

52

Ty looked at Dr. Moss.

"I had some popcorn that had a peanut butter taste. I didn't know it was peanut butter until it was in my mouth. I only had a little. But I guess it was enough to make me sick."

Dr. Moss stopped Ty.

"You had something else too, Ty. It reacted to the popcorn. The two things together made you sick."

Dr. Moss looked at the Koots. "We wouldn't have known about the peanut butter popcorn if Ty hadn't remembered. And Ty might not have remembered if he hadn't had time to think. And he wouldn't have had time to think if you guys hadn't been mad at him."

Dr. Moss went on. "We think something in the red sucker reacted to the popcorn. You boys wrote down everything Ty had that day. It helped the doctors a lot. You guys solved the mystery."

Ty looked at his friends.

54

"I still can't eat peanut butter. I still can't eat a lot of things. But now I know more things to be careful about.

"I don't ever want to be sick like that again," Ty said. "And I promise to never pretend to be sick."

He looked down. Then he looked at the Koots.

"Will you guys still be my friends?" he asked. He looked down again. He was afraid the Koots were going to say no. Ty took a deep breath. He hoped he wouldn't cry.

Toby, Abe, Ben, and Gabe looked at one another.

"We've always been your buds," Gabe said.

"We were just mad at you," Toby said.

"We just gave you some time out," Ben said. "We were going to start talking to you soon."

"Yeah," Abe said. "The Koots just didn't feel right without you."

Gabe gave Ty a friendly head rub. "Enough mush," he said. "If this is a party, where's the food?"

"You get to eat my food," Ty said. "Special cookies and juice. No peanut butter! No red suckers!"

"That's great," Toby said. "I'm not much of a PB & J fan anymore."

The Koots all agreed on that.

56